This book ~~belongs to~~ is controlled by

- -

For Mandy.

OXFORD
UNIVERSITY PRESS

Great Clarendon Street, Oxford OX2 6DP

Oxford University Press is a department of the University of Oxford.
It furthers the University's objective of excellence in research, scholarship, and
education by publishing worldwide.

Oxford is a registered trade mark of Oxford University Press in the UK and in
certain other countries

Text and illustrations © Richard Byrne 2016

The moral rights of the author/illustrator have been asserted Database right
Oxford University Press (maker)

First published in 2016

British Library Cataloguing in Publication Data
Data available

ISBN: 978-0-19-274629-0 (hardback)
ISBN: 978-0-19-274630-6 (paperback)

10 9 8 7 6 5 4 3 2 1

Printed in China

Paper used in the production of this book is a natural, recyclableproduct made
from wood grown in sustainable forests.The manufacturing process conforms to
the environmental regulations of the country of origin.

Visit www.richardbyrne.co.uk

Hoses and Ladders board-game included in this book!
If you would like to play hoses and ladders you just need a counter
for each player and a dice. Lie the book flat and take it in turns to
roll the dice. Move your counter forward the number of squares
shown on the dice. If your counter lands at the bottom of a ladder,
you can move up to the top of the ladder. If your counter lands on
the coiled end of a hose, you must slide down to the bottom of the
hose. The winner is the first player to reach the finish square.

BELLA'S STREET

This book is out of control!

Richard BYRNE

OXFORD
UNIVERSITY PRESS

Bella was at home when someone on the other page knocked at the door.

It was Ben.
He had a new toy to show Bella.

'It's remote controlled,' said Ben.
'Watch what the ladder does
when I press the UP button.'

But nothing seemed to happen. So Ben pressed the SPIN button.

'It's just not moving!' said Bella.
'See if it will make a noise instead.'
So Ben pressed the **SIREN** button.

'WOO-WOO!'

'It's a bit quiet,' said Bella.
'Try a different noise.
How about the **VOICE**
button?'

'Who said that?'
asked Bella.

'It's your dog!
He's talking!'
said Ben.

'I think **TURN** might work,' replied Ben.

But it didn't!
'Who's going to take control
of this book?' asked Bella.

'Oops!' said Ben.
'Well, it can't be me.'

Bella thought for a moment.
'Dear reader,' she began . . .

'it would be
lovely if you
could help us?'

'Try pressing the
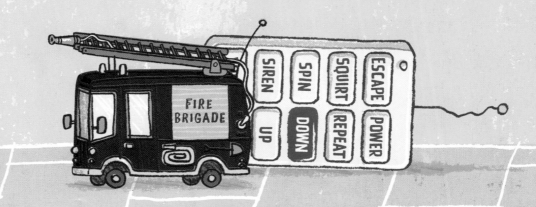 DOWN button!'
suggested Ben.

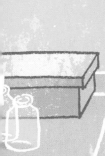

'Oh no, look!' said Bella.
'Are you sure you pressed
the right button?'

Ben was starting to feel a little queasy.

'Quick!' he burbled. 'Try the ESCAPE button.'

But things became even more muddled.

Dear reader,

Hold on tight!
Things are about to get . . .

. . . back under control? Phew!
To make sure, Bella's dog
clicked on the UP button.

It worked . . .

'I think your dog
has found the
SQUIRT button,'
said Ben.

Dear reader,
There's one button left to press. Can you find it?

See you again soon!

Bella Ben
x x

ESCAPE POWER
SQUIRT REPEAT
SPIN DOWN
SIREN UP
VOICE TURN

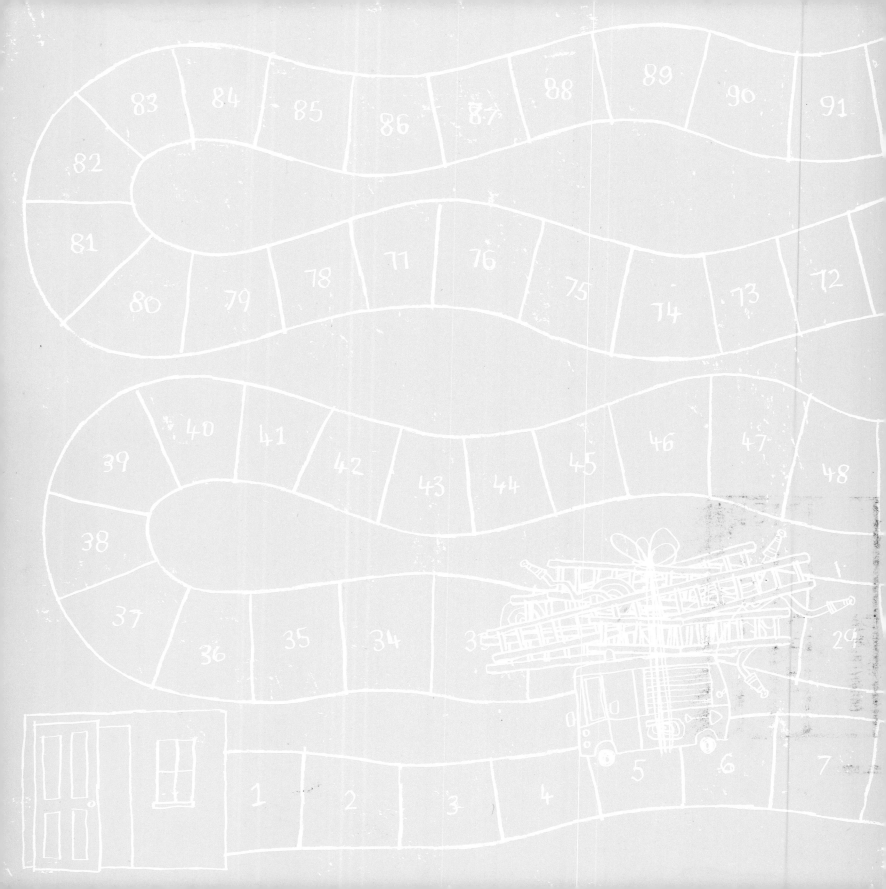